I0526894

Ceremonial Magick for Halfwits

Published by

DARKER INTENTIONS PRESS
POB 569
Freehold Township, New Jersey 07728-0569

All rights reserved. No part of this book may be reproduced in any form or by any means without prior written consent of the publisher, except in brief quotes for reviews.

If you purchased this book without a cover, you should be aware that this book is stolen property. It was reported "unsold and destroyed" to the publisher and neither the author or publisher has received any payment for this stripped "book."

This novelette is a complete work of fiction. Names, characters, places, and incidents are either the products of the author's imagination or are used fictitiously. Any resemblance to persons living or dead, or any events is pure coincidental.

PRINTED BY
Falcon Printing & Graphics
Freehold, New Jersey, USA

ISBN: 0-9769612-1-0

For more information on
DARKER INTENTIONS PRESS,
please visit us on the Web at:

www.darkerintentionspress.com
or contact jzdakota@hotmail.com

2005

The dragon opened its mouth and yawned, consciously letting the moonlight glint off his razor sharp teeth; I was supposed to be impressed. And indeed I was, as I felt a thin stream of urine running down my leg beneath my robe. If the dragon wanted to scare the piss out of me, he'd succeeded. What a fool I am! The only reason I'm standing here is because of a book I picked out of a sale bin called *Ceremonial Magick for Halfwits*.

All things considered the dragon was a magnificent creature, a three story tall beast, forty to fifty feet from his head to the tip of his tail. His massive back and chest were covered by scales, each about a foot long and blue-green. The dragon had a dished, horsy-looking face, but his huge lemon yellow eyes quickly reminded me that this creature was no Seabisquit. As smoke rings puffed out of his nose, the dragon bellowed in an unholy voice.

"And what name do you call yourself, wizard?"

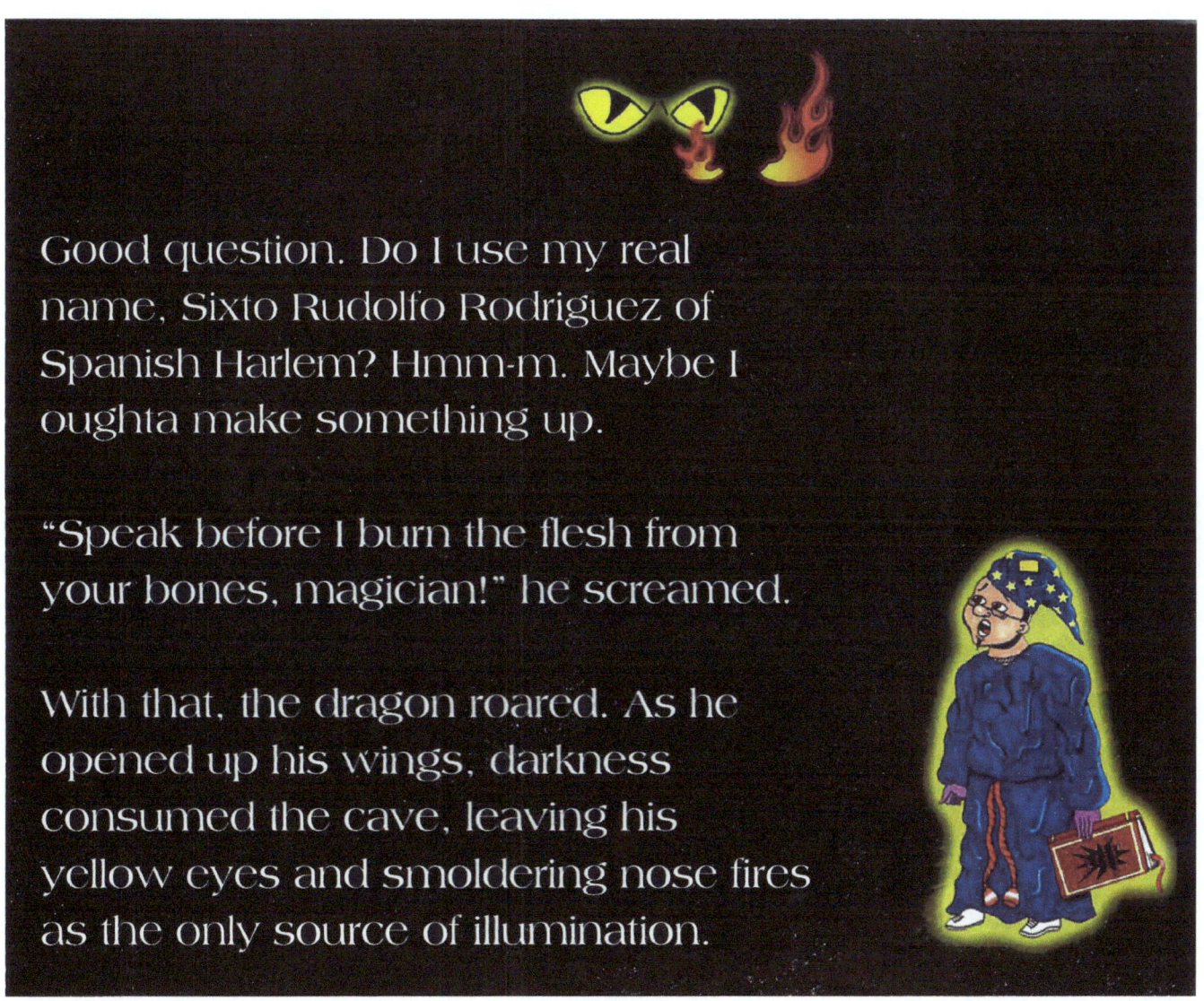

Good question. Do I use my real name, Sixto Rudolfo Rodriguez of Spanish Harlem? Hmm-m. Maybe I oughta make something up.

"Speak before I burn the flesh from your bones, magician!" he screamed.

With that, the dragon roared. As he opened up his wings, darkness consumed the cave, leaving his yellow eyes and smoldering nose fires as the only source of illumination.

My heart raced. What *do* I call myself? I hadn't gotten to the "anointing yourself with a sacred name" section of my book. Besides, all the good names like John Dee, Aleister Crowley, and Abramelin the Mage were already taken. I mentally ran through the list of things inside my medicine cabinet.

Ambience of Yonkers? Nah, sounded too French, and I didn't want him to know I had regular insomnia. The Great Pepsid of AC? Nah, sounded way too much like bicarbonate or a cheap Atlantic City lounge act. Finally, it struck

me. The little white pills in a dark brown glass bottle — the stuff my ex-wife took to prevent yeast infections.

"I am called Acidophilus of York Avenue, dragon." I stated proudly. "And your name?"

"Silence! Speak when you are spoken to, wretch!" the dragon said as it shoved its head in my face. "Master Acidophilus."

"Okay," I replied weakly.

"I am Talikon of a Thousand Fires. And now that you have disturbed my hundred year rest, what is it that you want oh great and terrible Acidophilus?" he laughed nastily.

Let me tell you… it's not easy being a half assed magician in the 21st Century.

I am a forty year old Puerto Rican man on a spiritual mission, a former neo-pagan, Rosicrucian, Hermetic magician and Santero all rolled up into one. I own a little bodega, a small Hispanic convenience store, on East 119th Street in Spanish Harlem, where I sell everything from Curse-Your-Neighbor spell kits to toilet paper and condoms. And for almost all of my life, I've been drawn to magic, though I don't know why. Everything I have ever conjured up has been a disaster.

Once I tried a simple money spell. Suddenly, a truck drove through the front window of my store. Eventually, I got money for the store damage through an insurance policy, but I nearly died in the process!

Another time I did an attraction spell during a waxing moon. Everything from feral dogs to old ladies wanted to consummate with me in the worst way. The most embarrassing episode occurred when I couldn't tear Loco, Mrs. Santiago's fifteen year old half dead Chihuahua, off my leg as he humped away doing seventy miles an hour. During the course of the act, old lady Santiago smiled at me and explained in a heavy Cuban accent, "Se-e-esto, when Loco gets the-es bothered, e-es always better to jus' leh he-e-em go."

And as if things weren't bad enough, my latest conjurations from *Ceremonial Magic for Halfwits* had gone awry...again. Using an ancient spell from the Keys of Solomon, I tried to conjure up some female companionship for the evening. But instead of getting a little mogambo with a Catherine Zeta-Jones clone, I'm about to become rump roast for Talikon.

"So I now ask you again, Great Acidophilus. Why have you disturbed me?"

"Eh, uh well, I was using the Keys of Solomon to conjure up a woman and, uh, you kinda showed up instead."

The dragon belly laughed at me. "Such magic!"

"Don't play with me Talikon!" I pulled out *Halfwits* and waived it in the air. "The Solomonic Keys are both holy and an infernal books!"

"Indeed," Talikon said patiently as he bent down and cocked his head. "Give me a display of your talents first," he hissed. "and then may be I will not eat you, wretch!"

"As you wish, Talikon. But be prepared for a major ass kickin'." I reached into the sleeve of my robe and removed my genuine, mail order, forty dollar, hazelwood wand imported from Scotland. After tracing an invisible pentagram in the air, I pointed the wand directly at Talikon's face and muttered some words in Latin as I visualized turning *him* into a pile of ash. The dragon's yellow eyes widened as I yelled, "*Damna in dupio inferno!*"

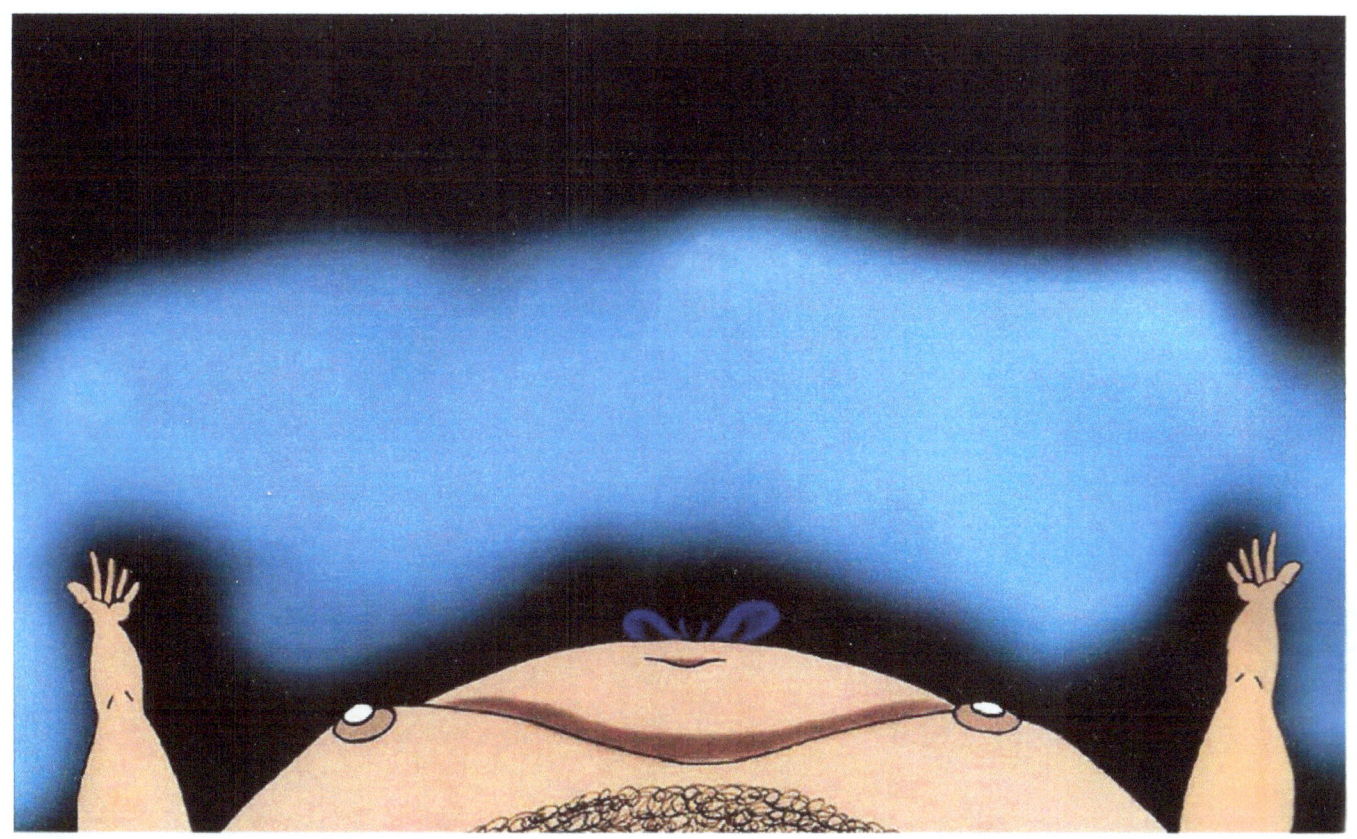

First, there was a puff of blue smoke. Nanoseconds later, I was completely naked. My hazelwood wand exploded into flames, right before it shriveled up and fell on the ground. As I looked down, I saw a blue satin bow dangling precariously from the very limp, un-magical wand attached to my groin.

First, Talikon chuckled. Then he made his giant claws into giant fists, and pounded the cavern floor as he simultaneously slapped it with his tail. Seconds later, small rocks fell from the ceiling as the great beast rolled on its back, howling with laughter. Skeletal remains of both men and animals fell on my head. I quickly dove for some sort of

cover, and finally hid behind a rock in case his lair collapsed. As tears of laughter poured down the beast's face, I watched with embarrassment, clad only in a blue ribbon. When the dragon finally regained his composure, he spoke.

"Master Acidophilus, you are an arse of a magician."

"A what?"

"An arse."

"What's an arse?"

"The back end of a mule, you fool!" he roared. "Och! Why am I wasting my bloody time with you?"

"You don't have to get nasty. Hey, I'm freezin'. You got any heat in here?"

In response, Talikon inhaled deeply, and blew a thin stream of fire upon a large rock. It became white hot and warmed the entire cavern. I sheepishly stood in front of this dragon-made heater with my "arse" facing Talikon while he looked on, apparently highly amused by the whole magical incident.

"You are a dabbler in magic. Am I not right?"

"Well, I practice but..."

"Ah, yes. practice. Sort of like a bad violinist. You practice and practice. and yet your playing pains even the ears of the patient angelus."

"Nobody likes a wordy dragon. Speak English."

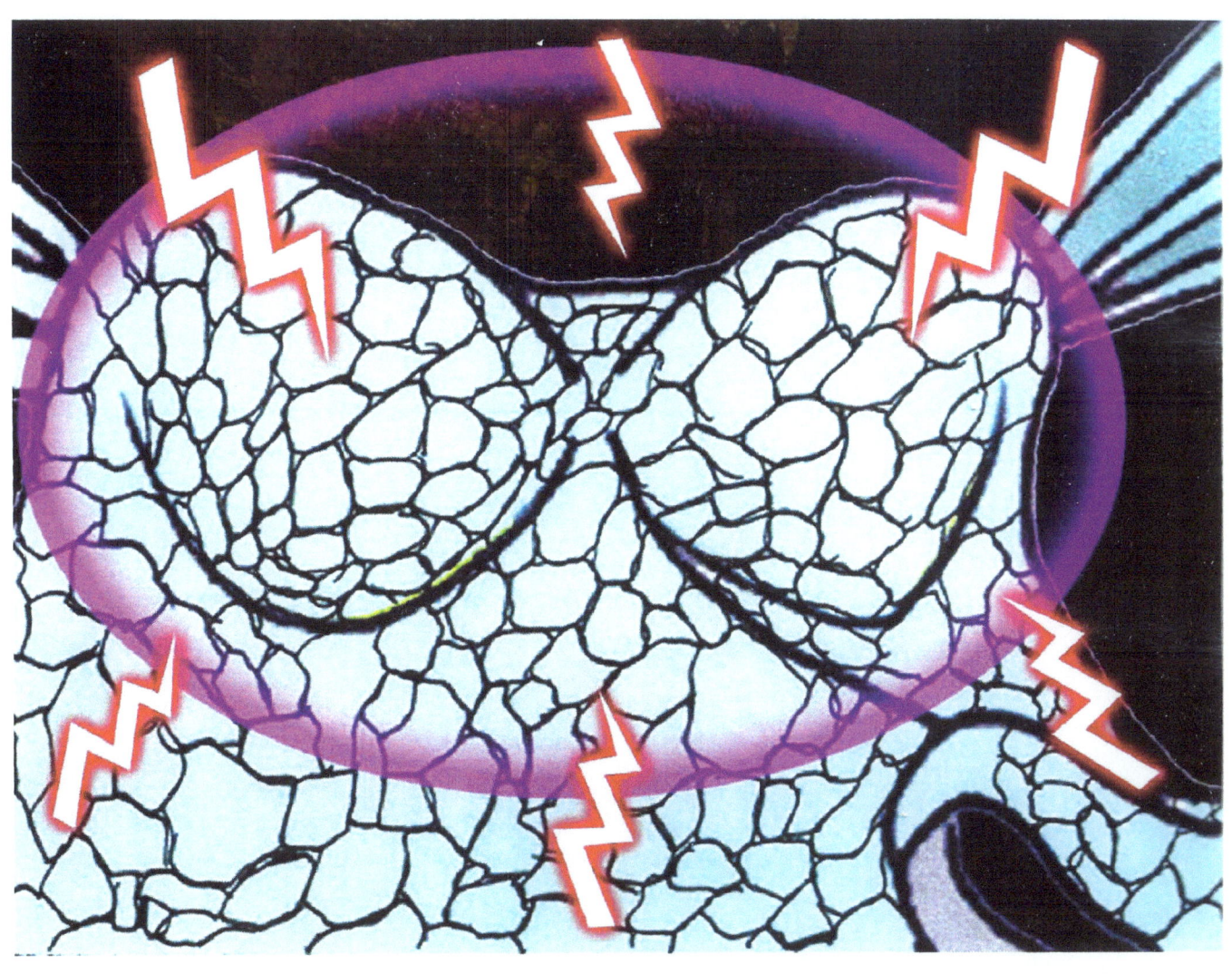

"I am English and one quarter Scot. Humans," he spat, "good for nothing alive, yet stringy when cooked. Ninnies, one and all." He sighed. "Magician, I tire of looking at your hairy naked arse." With that remark, Talikon blinked his eyes, and I was now fully clothed. Of course, I was dressed like a medieval bard, but at least Old Willie wasn't flying lonely in the breeze with a ribbon tied around his head.

"So, ah, how long have you been a dragon?" I thought maybe if I kept him talking he wouldn't kill me.

"It feels like a millennium."

"Get out of this cave much?"

"Not at all."

"Like your privacy?"

"Yes! Enough questions, magician!" Talikon turned around and stomped off in the other direction and dropped his head as he muttered, "How is it that you dare question me, wretch?"

"I was just trying to make conversation. I don't know anything about dragons. Well not really, I mean there's like Puff the Magic Dragon, Dragon flies, St. George killed a dragon…"

Talikon whipped around to face me again. "I hate the name George! To hell with St. George and anyone with that bloody name! He killed one of my great grandfathers five hundred years ago. Look, you are nothing more than an eejit which I shall have for my supper as soon as I tire of your senseless prattle."

"Okay, okay. So you want to eat me. That's cool. But before you turn me into a chicken fried steak, can you tell me where I am? Am I, like, back in the fifteenth century England or something?"

"You are right in your own time, foolish Acidophilus. My lair lies beneath a monastery in Fort Tryon Park. Surely you have heard of it, The Cloisters? The place has been around since 1914 which is how long I've been doomed to this place."

"You've been here since 1914?"

"Do not remind me again, but yes."

"How is it, like, no one's seen you? I mean look at you. You're as big as the cliff this whole place sits on. No one noticed you in 91 years? Not even those senior citizen bus tour groups that visit The Cloisters? Damn, Talikon, those old codgers never miss a trick."

"No one is permitted down this deep into The Cloisters. And besides I wasn't always this large."

"So how did you get here?"

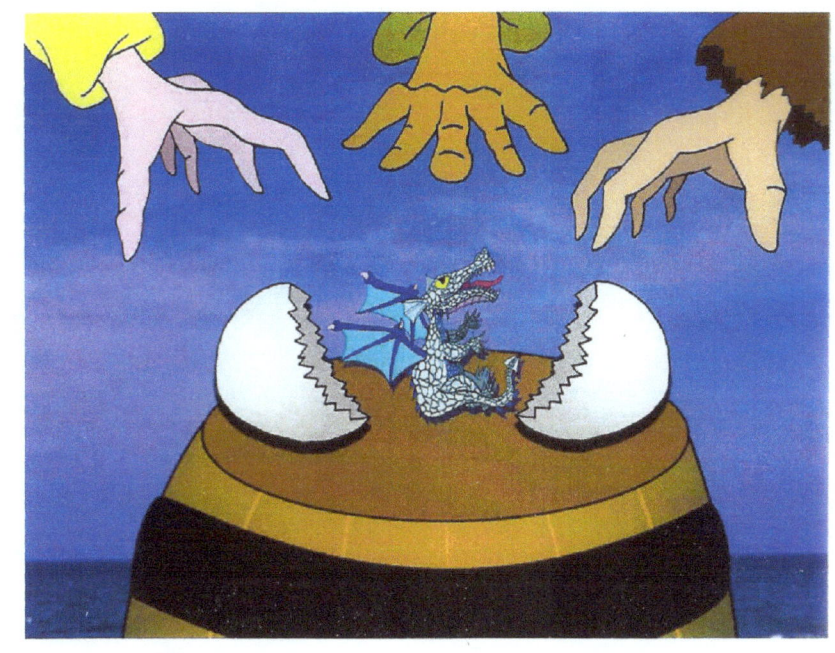

"I was accidently transported here by George Barnard in 1914 when he purchased a piece of a Gothic English Cathedral to build The Cloisters. I started to cross the sea as an egg. Half way during my passage, I hatched, and was given to Barnard by one of the seamen. When I was small and unobtrusive, I was a charming companion. But humans, so easily bored, found the need to dispatch me here once I didn't stop growing."

"Wow, man. You mean you were like, someone's pet?"

"Indeed."

"And here you are."

"Unfortunately, yes."

Despite his outward bravado, I saw

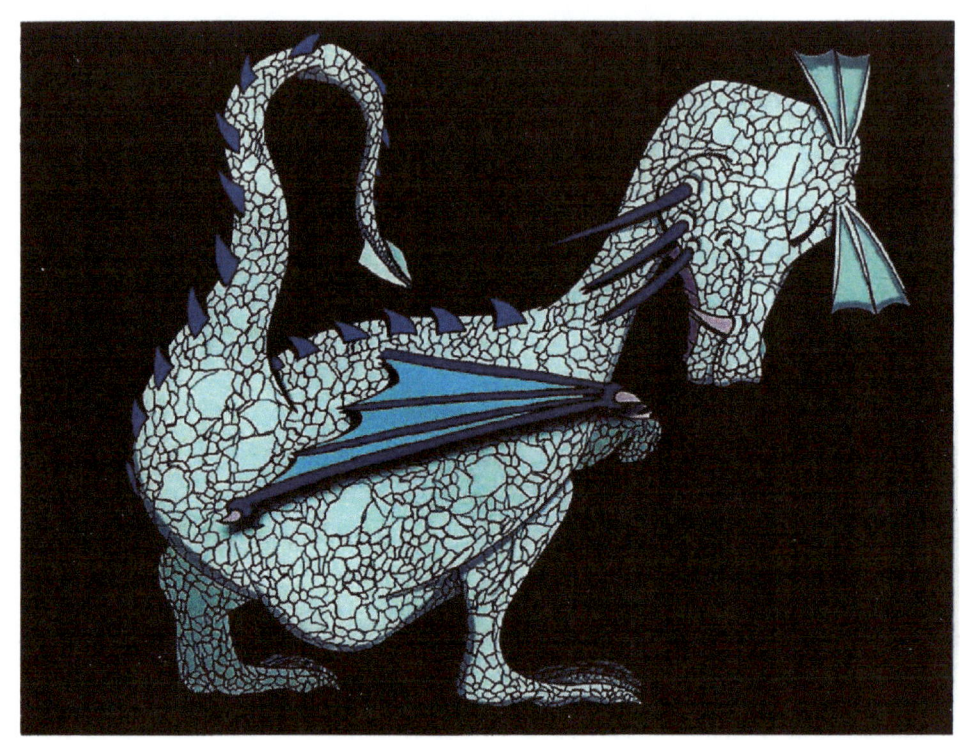

that this was one depressed dragon. For a split second, he reminded me of a tired, beaten down dog. I pitied him, then I mentally slapped myself remembering at any moment, I would be turned into an old fashioned Texas barbeque if he lost his temper.

"So, how is it that you couldn't escape? I mean just look at *you*. You could burn your way out of here."

"And where would I go? A zoo? A tawdry carnival? The world has no use for dragons anymore. And besides, I'm trapped here. Barnard had a friend who was a Master of the Dark Arts, a *real* magician, unlike you —"

"Thanks. Just stomp on my ego a little more."

"You vex me again and I will stomp on *you*, you sniveling, bald, porridged faced cur!" With that, Talikon slapped his tail against the cavern. Another human skull fell from the ceiling, cracking in half like an egg as it landed on my head.

"Ouch! Alright, alright. Calm down."

"Barnard's magician made a pact with the devil. As long as I stay sealed in The Cloisters, I will remain untouched and

fed human and animal flesh. But if I leave this place, I become a tithe to Hell and I will be collected by demons within two sunsets. A bit of a sticky wicket, yes?"

"The stickiest. But how would you get out of here given a choice?"

He sighed. "Let me show you."

I watched as Talikon raised his long neck and spread his wings. He roared at the top of his lungs. Once again, the cavern shook, while rocks and old bones clocked me on the head. For a minute, I thought it was some kind of illusion right before he dry gulched me like a hungry wolf. But when the smoke cleared, I was shocked.

If I could convince Talikon to leave the cave, this dude would be a helluva babe magnet for both of us. He stood over six feet tall with shoulder length brown hair, and he looked about thirty five years old. His eyes were the same blue green as his scales, but with a hint of dragon's fire gold. And if Talikon's dragon body was the pride of his species, his human physique wasn't far behind. He wore faded jeans, a black leather jacket, and sneakers. He coulda been a Calvin Klein model.

"Talikon, *amigo*! You old reptilian shape shifter! You are *mucho majo*! You ladykiller! Hang with me and you can get us both laid!"

He smiled. "Well, I say, it *has* been a long time since I have been with an attractive woman."

"One with or without scales?" I laughed. Talikon wasn't amused. Instead, he stared longingly at the cavern's exit. "I guess you're deciding what to do, right?"

"I *have* decided what to do, Acidophilus. Before the second sunset comes, you will be my guide to the living world. When my time is done, you are free to go and I will meet my fate. Come, let us go forth into the human world."

"I thought you hated humans."

"I do. But I never said your species wasn't interesting. Time is short. Hurry along."

"Okay, but one thing. Can you fix my clothes? I mean this bard outfit is a great look for reading poetry in an East Village café, but it won't get over in my neighborhood, if you know what I mean."

Talikon closed his eyes and I found myself back in modern day street clothes. "Follow me through that doorway, Acidophilus."

"Hey listen. Just call me Sixt. Everybody does. But we gotta get you a new name."

"I have a fine old family name. What is the matter with it?" He stated flatly.

24

"Oh yeah, right. A fine old family name if you're a mythical British lizard. Talikon alone won't cut it here. This is 2005. I'm going to call you, Tommy or something. Now that works. Tommy Talikon. Very cool. Very happening, particularly with that English accent thing you got working. Makes you sound like a rock star or something. American females die for that English accent."

"I will answer to the name of Thomas, not Tommy." The dragonman replied. "Come. I wish to see the city lights one last time."

To get him out of the mainstream, I brought Tommy the Dragonman home and introduced him to my sister, Maria. When they looked at each other, I knew there would be problems. They immediately fell head over heels in love. At Thomas demand, the three of us ran around New York City

eating, drinking and dancing our asses off at night, while we did the tourist thing during the day. Thomas had a particular fondness for the medieval art

section of The Metropolitan Museum of Art, mainly because he recognized half of the dragons in the paintings as some distant relative or other.

I'll tell you, dragon-boy was so good looking, women on the street just stopped and stared at him. And me? Well, like the hungry dog hiding under the table at dinner time, I caught Thomas' lady leftovers, many of which laughed at me and walked away when I tried to

pass myself off as his twin, separated from birth, Puerto Rican brother from the U.K.

Maria was totally charmed by this strange Englishman with a body like Adonis and the gentle face of a poet. And he couldn't take his eyes off my sister, which made me both happy and worried. After all, my dragonman, was living on borrowed time so to speak. He'd be gone by dark, and Maria's heart would be broken—again.

Finally, when the sky turned a peculiar shade of grey and a crack of thunder rolled around inside of the clouds, Thomas and I looked at each other. We both knew it was time for him to go.

"Sixt, I would have one small glass of port before I leave."

"No problem, amigo."

My sister threw her arms around Thomas' neck. "You're not going anywhere."

Thomas looked at me and then looked back at my sister. For once, the big mouth dragon was at a complete loss for words. " Love, I cannot stay with you anymore. I have to go back."

I interjected. "Yeah, Maria, see uh, what Tommy didn't tell you is that, uh, well his, uh, visa, yeah, that's right, visa, ran out and he's about to be deported. He's gotta get on a plane back to England. Tonight." I watched Thomas hold Maria as she cried. They both looked *really* sad. But there wasn't anything anyone could do.

As I looked across Sixth Avenue, I noticed two armed Immigration and Customs Enforcement Officers ascending the subway. The men stood across the street

staring at us with their arms folded. They looked like normal federal agents until one of them smiled, revealing a skeletal mouth with bloody fangs. The larger of the two waived a set of handcuffs in the air and pointed to us.

"They're here, Sixt. It is time. Take care of Maria for me."

"I'm going with you, Thomas. I won't leave you." I watched Maria wrap her arounds him tighter.

The dragonman gently handed me my sister. "Take this precious woman before she gets hurt."

"Okay, Tommy. I can do that. Wait, I have an idea. Let me go with you."

"Sixt, what is it you think you can do? These are not low ranking infantry men. They are infernal royalty."

"Would one of you please tell me what the hell is happening?" Maria cried.

"Later, Maria. This is complicated, very, very complicated. Just stay here on this side of the street and let me straightened this out. Trust me?" I said smiling nervously as I patted her cheek. "Yo, dragonboy, follow me."

Together we walked across the street and I greeted the demons. "Evening gents."

The first demon officer hissed. "Are you the man-dragon?"

"No. I am Talikon of a Thousand Fires." Thomas shoved his wrists forward to be cuffed. "I am your servant now."

I place my hand over his wrists. "Not so fast dragonboy. You 're *my* servant. I found you first."

Thomas looked flabbergasted. "What are you doing?"

I looked directly into the demon's red soulless eyes. "I found him first. So if you want the dragon, you'll have to fight me for him."

31

The second demon laughed and grabbed my collar as he lifted me off the ground. "I can rip your throat out right here, toss the contents of your stomach on the pavement and make your dead grandmother lick up the remains. Who are you to challenge us?" he growled.

"I am the Great Magician Acidophilus of York and I have this." I promptly pulled out the damn book that got me into trouble in the first place—*Ceremonial Magic for Halfwits.*

Thomas' palm struck his forehead in disgust. "Eejit! Bloody hell, you shall kill us both!"

Ignoring dragonman's snide comment, I noticed the amulets around the demons' wrists. I turned right to the chapter on demon identification. According to *Halfwits*, these amulets were infernal identification bracelets, revealing the rank of the spirit in Hell's corporate hierarchy.

"Hmm, let's see," I said studying the bracelet. "You're the Great infernal Marquis Magotz. It says here that you 'can appear in any form. " 'Generally has a living tattoo of a snake on his body'," I said looking at the tattoo of an asp wiggling on his bicep. "Okay yeah, I see the tattoo. You're definitely Marquis Magotz. You generally travel with and do the bidding of Verintz, an infernal Duke. Okay, it says 'generally Verintz, appears as a green faced, snaggle-toothed old sea hag, but can appear in pleasing form if needed'. Hey wait! You're Verintz, his boss, right? Cool! How long you two been doin' the soul collecting gig together?"

"Enough!" hissed Magotz. "We have no business with you." He smiled sinisterly as he twisted his head around in a complete circle. "At least, not while you are still alive."

"Sixt, you gone bloody mad! Let them just take me! It is over!"

"Quiet dragon breath! I ain't done with my demon boys here."

"So I'll wager my soul for dragon-breath's over here. My magic beats your magic and I keep the dragon. Deal?"

"Let me understand your terms, wizard." Duke Verintz laughed. "You perform an act of magic. Your act of magic, as you say, beats mine, and you keep the dragon."

"Yup."

"And if your act of magic fails, we get your soul as well as the dragon's."

"That's the deal. You in, boys?"

Duke Verintz chortled as he looked at Magotz. "Clearly a proposition we cannot refuse. What will be your act of magic? Shape shift into a thousand bats? Cloud the moon with the souls of a thousand dead Roman warriors? Part the Red Sea, perhaps? Let me say this: it's been done. All rather unimpressive if you ask me."

"Nope. I simply ain't that fancy. I'm just a little Puerto Rican boy from Manhattan."

"Well, what then?" asked Verintz.

"Inspect my deck of cards, Magotz."

Magotz looked over at his boss. "My Lord?"

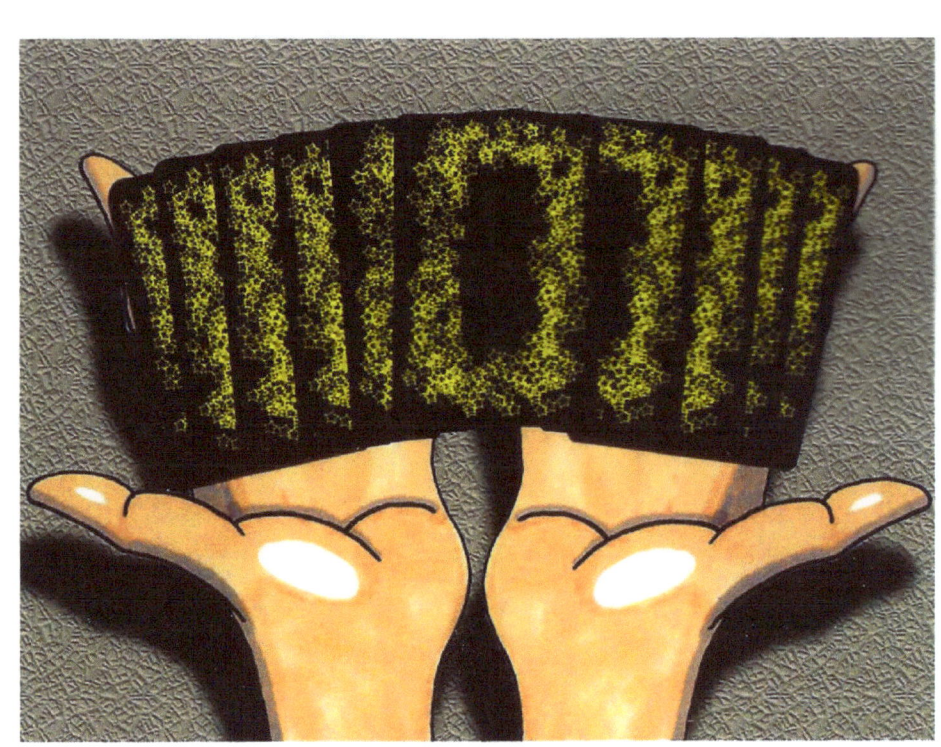

"Just do it Magotz, so we can get out of here." Verintz ordered.

"Are the suits all different?"

Magotz went through the whole deck and nodded at me. "Yes, Spades, Hearts, Clubs and Diamonds. "

"Pick a card."

I looked at Thomas. His mouth had dropped open. I didn't know if he going to pass out or punch me in the head. The demon picked a card.

"Now look at the card," I cautioned, "don't tell me what it is, just stick it back in the deck. Then I will tell you what card you picked."

The demon looked at the card and returned it to the deck. "Done, wizard. What was my card?"

"Ten of Diamonds, Magotz."

Duke Verintz laughed. "Allow me get the other set of cuffs ready. A good day's work Marquis Magotz. We come for one soul and we collect two. His Dark Majesty will be pleased. Tell us all what suit the card really was."

Magotz snorted. "The bastard magician was right. It was the Ten of Diamonds."

Like psychotic snakes, Verintz and Magotz began

hissing wildly at Thomas and me. Then they descended back into the underground shadows of the subway, cursing in some of the foulest language I'd ever heard.

"It isn't over Acidophilus! Wait till you die!" yelled Verintz as he pointed at me. "I will come for you, myself!"

I smiled and waived back at the two fading demonic agents. "I'll be taking my dragon now. *Adios*, losers."

Thomas turned to me. "Thank you. I misjudged you, Sixt. You truly are a wondrous magician."

"Hey, anybody can be a good street magician with this deck." I showed him the other side of my card deck where every card was the Ten of Diamonds.

By now, Maria raced across the street, borderline hysterical. "Will someone please tell me what's going on?"

"*Calma hermanita,*. Those nice ICE agents made a mistake about my English boy here. His visa is cool, so I think he'll be hanging around—."

Before I could finish the sentence Thomas and Maria were lip locked like a couple of lovesick lampreys. Tommy really *had* been trapped in that cave 91 years too long. Once he came up for air, Thomas smiled and looked over my sister's shoulder. He winked at me.

I rubbed my hands together. "Okay, Tommy. Now it's payback time."

"What can I do for you, my friend?"

"First, you gotta let some of that English accent rub off on me. Babes get hot over that accent even if it's from an ugly guy. Oh yeah, and you gotta teach me some real magic, like that shape shifting trick you did in the cave."

Thomas the dragonman shook his head in disbelief. "Sixt, you are already a bit of a lad, with your fine Spanish-

American accent. And magic? You do not need my help with magic. You possess that wonderful book."

"Not anymore." I announced. With an ear to ear grin I tossed *Ceremonial Magic for Halfwits* down the nearest sewer grate. "Why do I need a book when I got me a *real* magic teacher?"

From the worried look on the Tommy Talikon's face, I could see that the smelly old cave beneath The Cloisters looked real good to him right about now.

Acknowledgments:

From the Author: Many thanks to my husband for his good humor and patience, to Maria Taktikos for her pictures of The Cloisters, and to my friend Terrie Hunt who always enjoyed a good laughing dragon. This book could not have been possible without help from Ms. Elaine at Falcon Printing in Freehold, New Jersey.

From the Illustrator, Vincent Lisa: I would like to give a special thanks to Peggy Matikonis for working providing me with a wonderful opportunity to work on this book. I also want to thank my friends and family for their love, support, and for being my biggest inspirations throughout my life.

www.ingramcontent.com/pod-product-compliance
Lightning Source LLC
Chambersburg PA
CBHW041720240626

47171CB00002B/10